EMMA
by James Stevenson

GREENWILLOW BOOKS

NEW YORK

Library of Congress Cataloging in Publication Data
Stevenson, James, (date) Emma.
Summary: With the help of her friends, and after a few false
starts, a young witch named Emma learns to fly on her broom.
[1. Witches—Fiction.   2. Flight—Fiction] I. Title.
PZ7.S84748Em   1985   [E]   84-4141
ISBN 0-688-04020-9   ISBN 0-688-04021-7 (lib. bdg.)